GREMLINS 2

THE NEW BATCH

Gizmo's Great Escape

By Justine Korman
Illustrated by Gene Biggs & Kim Ellis

A GOLDEN BOOK • NEW YORK
Western Publishing Company, Inc., Racine, Wisconsin 53404

TM & © 1990 Warner Bros. Inc. All rights reserved. Printed in the U.S.A. No part of this book may be reproduced or copied in any form without written permission from the publisher. GOLDEN, GOLDEN & DESIGN, GOLDENCRAFT, A GOLDEN BOOK, A GOLDEN LOOK-LOOK BOOK, and A GOLDEN LOOK-LOOK BOOK & DESIGN are trademarks of Western Publishing Company, Inc. Library of Congress Catalog Card Number: 89-81970 ISBN: 0-307-12590-4/ISBN: 0-307-66590-9 (lib. bdg.)
A B C D E F G H I J K L M

Gizmo hummed a happy tune in his cozy cage. The Mogwai was the greatest curiosity in Mr. Wing's Chinatown curiosity shop. There, Gizmo could get out of his unlocked cage whenever he liked.

Old Mr. Wing coughed as he played chess with himself. He paused and hissed, "Shhh. Strangers are coming."

Gizmo knew he would have to hide. He peeked through his cage as four grim-looking men in business suits climbed out of a big black limousine. They carried a television set and a VCR into Mr. Wing's store. Gizmo wondered what they were doing.

"Mister Wing? Daniel Clamp would like to speak to you," said Forster, the sour-faced leader, while the other men set up the TV and the VCR.

The TV screen flashed to life with a videotape of the real estate tycoon Daniel Clamp. Mr. Clamp had already bought all the other buildings on Mr. Wing's block, and he was determined to buy Mr. Wing's building, too.

Mr. Clamp made a very pushy speech, offering Mr. Wing lots of money. He wanted to tear down the shop to build the Clamp Chinatown Centre, a huge modern office complex.

"Two people can always agree," Clamp's image insisted.

Mr. Wing said, "I'm sorry. Please tell Mr. Clamp the answer is no."

"Keep the TV," said Forster, leaving with his men.

Mr. Wing coughed again.

"Tee vee!" Gizmo exclaimed. He wondered why Mr. Wing wasn't happy about the wonderful present.

"Television!" Mr. Wing exclaimed, switching off the set. "An invention for fools." He coughed again. Gizmo knew his old friend was worried about something else, and he felt sad because Mr. Wing was very ill.

"Mr. Wing's death removes the last obstacle to developer
Daniel Clamp's Chinatown project..." a TV reporter
announced a few days later.

Gizmo was lonely, sitting in his cage, a black armband
around one fuzzy arm. He missed Mr. Wing very much.
Gizmo switched off the TV and sang a sad song.

Suddenly there was a loud crash. A bulldozer smashed the
front of Mr. Wing's store. A terrified Gizmo jumped out of
his cage. He scrambled into the side alley as the store
collapsed in a heap of plaster and wood. Gizmo looked back at
the wreckage. He had escaped just in time.

Panting, Gizmo ran through the dirty alley. He felt all alone in the world, without friends or a home. But before he could catch his breath, Gizmo was grabbed by two human hands.

Gizmo was taken to a laboratory full of unhappy animals and strange gadgets. Big men in white coats were peering down at Gizmo through the bars of his cage.

"Say, Dr. Catheter, look at this," said a scientist named Lewis.

"Some sort of rodent, apparently," Martin, another scientist, observed.

"It can't take bright light," Lewis added.

"Watch this," said Martin, switching on some music and opening Gizmo's cage. The Mogwai danced to the bouncy beat.

"Hmph! Cute, isn't he?" Dr. Catheter said grumpily.

Gizmo danced as the men talked. Each hop took him farther from his cage, and Gizmo hoped to slip away.

But Dr. Catheter grabbed Gizmo and stuffed him back into his cage. "What's wrong with you two?" he asked Lewis and Martin. "He almost escaped! How are you proceeding with this specimen?"

Lewis said, "Cell samples tomorrow..."

"...tissue cultures Thursday," Martin finished.

"And then body structure," Catheter said, poking the frightened Mogwai.

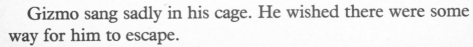

Gizmo sang sadly in his cage. He wished there were some way for him to escape.

Just then a messenger delivered a package to Dr. Catheter.

"This is rabies," Catheter complained. "I was supposed to get the flu this week."

Gizmo wished they would all get the flu and leave him alone. The messenger left, whistling Gizmo's tune.

In the same building, Gizmo's friend, Billy Peltzer, was talking to his girlfriend, Kate, on the video phone. They both missed the good old days in Kingston Falls, before the Gremlin attack. Billy felt out of place in the super-modern Clamp Centre, where he and Kate now worked. Just then the lights went out and came back on again, and the phone went dead. Nothing was working properly in the building.

In the sudden silence, Billy heard Gizmo's song.

Billy turned and saw the messenger who had been at the lab.

"Where did you hear that song?" Billy asked him excitedly.

The messenger thought for a minute, then remembered. "Somebody was humming it in the Splice-O-Life Lab on the eighteenth floor."

Billy knew right away who had been humming—Gizmo!
He thought of his poor little friend in the genetics lab and
realized he had to rescue him.

By pretending to be a repairman, Billy managed to get into
the laboratory.

While he fiddled with one of the machines, Billy whistled
Gizmo's song. The lab was a scary-looking place filled with
weird scientists performing strange experiments. Billy listened
carefully for an answer to his song. He hoped he wasn't too late.

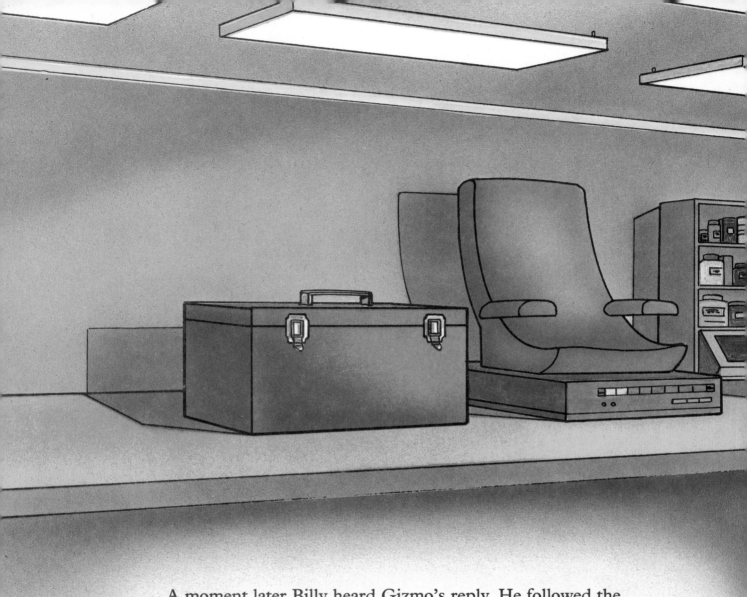

A moment later Billy heard Gizmo's reply. He followed the sound of Gizmo's voice, past the busy scientists and cages of chattering monkeys.

When Billy finally found Gizmo's cage, he was so relieved. He had to get his friend out of there right away.

Billy strolled back to the machine he had pretended to be fixing. On the way, he unlatched the monkey cages. The mischievous monkeys rushed out and started wrecking the lab. The frantic scientists had their hands full trying to recapture the animals.

Billy's plan worked. In all the confusion, the scientists didn't see Billy unlock Gizmo's cage and scoop the Mogwai into his big red toolbox.

Billy's heart was pounding as he slipped out of the lab, leaving the broken machine in pieces.

He tried to look cool, even though he expected to get caught at any moment.

Once outside the lab, Billy took Gizmo out of the toolbox.

"Hey, guy, did you miss me?" Billy asked, happy that his little friend was safe and sound.

Gizmo hugged Billy. He was free and reunited with his friend. No matter what happened, they would be together.